For Rory, Peter and Brian

Philomel Books
Published by the Penguin Group
Penguin Group (USA) LLC
375 Hudson Street, New York, NY 10014

USA | Canada | UK | Ireland | Australia | New Zealand | India | South Africa | China
penguin.com   A Penguin Random House Company

Library of Congress Cataloging-in-Publication Data is available upon request.

Manufactured in China.

Package ISBN 978-0-399-17109-3
20 19 18 17 16 15 14 13 12 11

Lost and Found

Oliver Jeffers

PHILOMEL BOOKS

Once there was a boy

who found a penguin at his door.

The boy didn't know where it had come from,

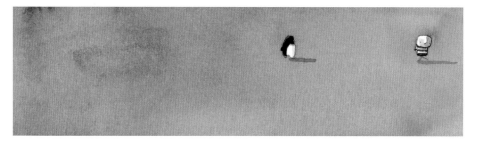

but it began to follow him everywhere.

The penguin looked sad and
the boy thought it must be lost.

So the boy decided to help the penguin
find its way home.

He checked in the Lost and Found Office.
But no one was missing a penguin.

He asked some birds if they knew
where the penguin came from.

But they ignored him.
Some birds are like that.

The boy asked his duck.

But the duck floated away.
He didn't know either.

That night, the boy couldn't sleep for disappointment. He wanted to help the penguin but he wasn't sure how.

The next morning he discovered that
penguins come from the South Pole.
But how could he get there?

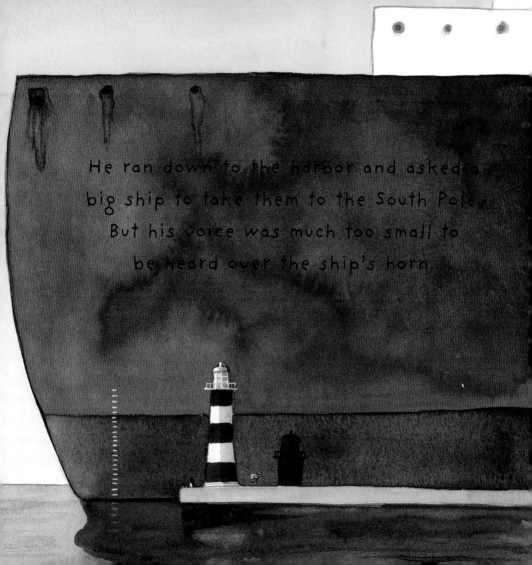

He ran down to the harbor and asked a big ship to take them to the South Pole. But his voice was much too small to be heard over the ship's horn.

Together, the boy decided, he and the penguin would row to the South Pole. So the boy took his rowboat out and tested it.

He told stories to the penguin to help pass the time.

They packed everything they would need
and pushed the rowboat out to sea.

They rowed south for many days . . .

. . . and many nights.
There was lots of
time for stories, and the
penguin listened to every one,
so the boy would always
tell another.

They floated through good weather and bad,

when the waves were as big as mountains.

Until, finally, they came to the South Pole.

The boy was delighted,
but the penguin said nothing.
Suddenly it looked sad again as
the boy helped it out of the boat.

The boy said good-bye . . .

. . . and floated away. When he looked back,
the penguin was still there.
But it looked sadder than ever.

It felt strange for the boy
to be on his own.

There was no point telling stories now
because there was no one to listen.

Instead, he just thought.

And the more he thought . . .
the more he realized
he had made a big
mistake.

The penguin hadn't been lost.
It had just been lonely.

Quickly he turned the boat around
and rowed back to the South Pole
as fast as he could.

At last he reached
the Pole again . . .
But where was
the penguin?

The boy searched
and searched, but
he was nowhere
to be found.

Sadly, the boy set off for home.

But then the boy saw something
in the water ahead of him.

Closer and closer he got,
until he could see . . .

. . . the penguin!

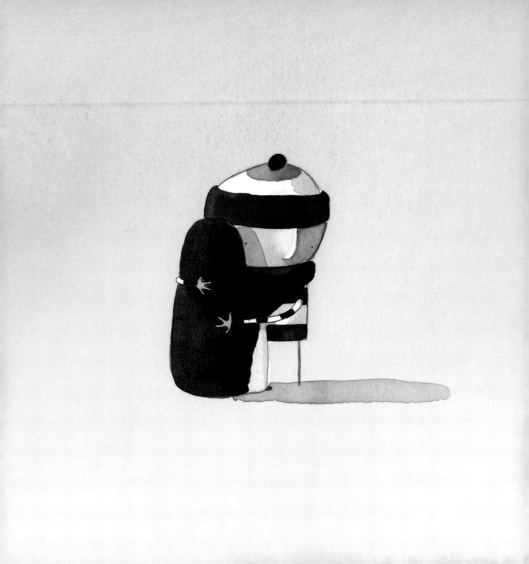

And so the boy and his friend went home together, talking of wonderful things all the way.